Making of Champions

Author
Beth Watter

Table of Contents

Dedication

This book, *Champions, in Training*, is being dedicated to Bob Bartwell. We call him Bart. He is a great Champion. Not only does he win races on his bike, but his life is an example of what a champion should be and do.

Bart created a summer camp that changes people's lives. He is a role model for every person, showing them, through his life's example, how to overcome challenges and become champions.

His amazing faith and love make him draw people to him. Everyone who attends his camp wants to make him proud. His encouragement makes every boy or girl, man or woman want to be the best they can be.

Every year that Nik has gone to Ironwood Springs Summer Camp, he has come home stronger and more independent.

Bart went to Heaven recently. We know he went to Heaven because his faith, love, and loving compassion made him an angel to us here on earth.

Lord, please take good care of our friend until we see him again.

Acknowledgment

This book has only been possible because of my amazing husband.

Thank you, Klaus, for giving me the freedom and strength to be Nik's mom.

Thank you for supporting me through all our tough times.

I may have lost you before I finished my book, but I could have only done this because you gave us everything you had until your last breath.

Thank you to my friends and family, who have kept me moving forward.

Thank you, Rick, for encouraging me to finish what I started.

1

"Holy smokes! I want to do that! Matt, what do you think? That would be so much fun! Do you think we can talk our parents into letting us go to Minnesota?"

Matt laughed at Nik's excitement. "Well, I guess we'll have to get more details before we ask. You know they'll have a lot of questions."

As Nik rolled towards home, his mind was racing. Maybe he could take his new, red racing bike. He remembered seeing on the video that camp started each year with the Chariots of Fire Race. What a blast it would be to be with other racers, flying down the road.

A Wheelchair Sports Camp! Everyone would be in wheelchairs. It looked like they were trying just about any sport they wanted. He remembered watching them play baseball, basketball, tennis, and so much more. They even had horseback riding!

When Nik rolled into the house, no one was home.

Oh, good grief! He was bursting with excitement to tell someone about Ironwood Springs.

Josh answered on the first ring. "Hey, buddy!" Nik said. "Can you come over? I have some exciting news to share."

"Okay," Josh mumbled as he finished his sandwich. "Be right there! Let me finish my milk."

By the time Josh showed up, Nik had his computer set up and was ready to play the video.

Just as Josh came through the door, Nik's parents arrived.

"Well, guys! What's happening?"

Nik's Dad asked as he set down a bag of groceries. He could see how excited Nik was.

"Mom and Dad, do you have a few minutes to watch a video?

Matt and I watched it earlier. I really want you to see it."

Nik's Mom quickly put the cold things in the fridge and joined the boys in the family room.

"What has you so excited, Nik?"

"Matt and I were at the park. We watched a kid fly by us on a blue racing bike, like my red one. He circled around and came back to talk with us. He was telling us that he was practicing to race in the Chariots of Fire."

Dad watched Nik turn on the computer with curiosity. "I haven't heard of this race, Nik. Where is it held?"

When the video started, everyone stopped talking. All eyes were on the racing bikes and wheelchairs. Every face in the race was smiling and laughing.

Nik smiled. He was pretty sure that his family was just as impressed with the Wheelchair Sports Camp as he was.

"Well, Dad! I have to find out more details and facts. Then Matt and I and Josh, if he wants, need to set up a meeting to share the information. I think we would all love attending this camp."

Mom and Dad watched as Nik and Josh went out to the deck to talk. "My goodness!" Mom spoke softly. "Can you imagine what Nik could learn and accomplish at a camp like that? I think our little boy is quickly growing into a smart, young man."

"The only thing that concerns me," Dad said. "A camp like that has to be really expensive. And how far away it might be. I know I haven't heard of anything like that nearby."

"The boys made money shredding paper. Maybe they can pay some. I'll have to check with Nik. I haven't seen him spending very much. Other than his bike, I think most of his money may have gone into his savings."

"That would sure help," said Dad. "I would hate for him to miss something like this, because we couldn't afford it."

"Don't worry, sweetheart!" Mom smiled. "If it's important to the boys, they will find a way to make it happen."

Nik called through the door, "Hey, Mom, we're going to the park. Maybe we'll run into our friends. It would be great if a few more guys wanted to go to camp. Come on, Josh!"

"Nik, how much do you think this will cost? My Dad won't be happy if I ask for a lot of money."

"Josh, don't you remember that we have a bank account? We saved most of the money from our shredding paper. I bought my bike, you went to Football Camp, and Matt put money into his car."

"We all put half our money into our bank account," Nik laughed. "We are in good shape. Every week when we shred paper, our account grows. I don't think that we will have any problem paying for camp."

"What a relief. Do you think we should tell our parents how much money we have? It's not really a secret. They just haven't asked."

"If they ask, by all means, we'll tell them," said Nik. "We haven't needed to spend a lot. I guess when we pay for camp ourselves, that will open up that conversation."

2

Matt thought he was the first to arrive for the planning meeting. He still got a real kick out of driving his car. Having it set up to meet his special needs was the best graduation gift he had received.

His Grandfather had known exactly what would make him happy again. Matt had thought he'd never drive again after his football accident. But now he laughed every time he got behind the wheel.

"Hey, Matt! Where's your folks? Josh and his parents are already inside." Nik rolled out to watch Matt unload and climb into his new, lightweight sports chair.

Spinning his chair, before heading up the ramp, showed how well Matt had adjusted and learned to enjoy life again.

"They'll be here. I just wanted to drive myself. I still can't believe how much freedom my car gives me. I feel alive again!"

Matt's parents arrived just as the boys opened the front door. Nik waited at the door for them. "Thanks for coming! We have a lot to talk about."

Nik had invited their new friend, Doug, to come, also. He thought that since Doug had attended camp a few times, he would be able to answer a lot of questions.

Matt and Nik sat in front of the group. Nik started off by introducing Doug to everyone.

Doug had brought along his photo album and brochures from camp. And, he wore a very cool t-shirt with the Chariots of Fire Race on the back.

After looking through the pictures and materials from camp, there were a lot of questions.

"Okay, guys," Nik's Dad said. "This looks like an amazing camp, but where is it and how much does it cost?"

Matt rolled over with a brand new Travel Atlas. As he opened it up to Minnesota, he had everyone's attention. As he pointed out where the camp was, he said, "I think we can drive up there in about five hours."

"We can drive right up this side of the Mississippi to La Crosse, Wisconsin. We can cross the river at that big bridge. We can drive right to Rochester, which is right by Stewartville."

"Wait a minute, let me think about this for a minute," Matt's Dad said. "That's a long drive for you guys to go alone the first time. I think maybe we parents might like to see this amazing camp and meet the staff."

"If you plan to take your chairs, bikes, and other stuff, we might want to invite your Grandfather to bring his van. I bet he will be very impressed with this Wheelchair Sports Camp. I think it would be a nice surprise for him."

Matt laughed. "Gramps is going to be so impressed that we found such a cool camp without his help."

"Okay, guys!" Nik's Mom said. "I called the camp. You have two weeks to get organized. But your registration has to get in immediately. Did you boys save any money from your paper shredding? Luckily this camp is half the price of all the other camps around here. But you will need $250 each. You have to send it, with your registrations."

Nik laughed, "We knew we wanted to do something special this year. So we put money in the bank every week. We have more than enough for camp. We are planning for our future, you know. Every week, our account grows. We are learning by following your examples."

"Boys," Josh's Dad said, "You have impressed me again. Nik, I think you are good for Josh. He has never been good with money. Maybe you are all going to be well-balanced adults."

"Dad, I am really trying to handle money better. Nik and Matt both have convinced me to look to the future and plan ahead."

Doug cleared his throat. "If you are all in agreement, this should be an awesome week at camp. I need to get home. I still have a lot to do before going to camp. Thanks for letting me share my experiences."

"Thanks, Doug! I think you have given these young men a great new adventure for the summer," Matt's Dad said with a laugh. "I remember the days of you guys just running and playing and having water fights. Life was simpler. But, watching you guys grow into thinking, hardworking young men, makes me very proud."

3

Nik, Matt, Josh, and Doug all arrived at Ironwood Springs like a caravan. Each family parked and waited.

As they entered the beautiful log structure, everyone looked around in amazement. The building was huge, and the hallways were wide, leading to the bedrooms with private bathrooms, large meeting rooms, and game rooms.

You might think you had stepped into a very nice, rustic resort. What a beautiful camp!

Every building, every walkway, the petting zoo, and the miniature golf course were totally accessible.

When they met Bob Bardwell, they understood the perfectly planned camp. The Director was in a wheelchair, himself.

This was his dream.

"Mr. Bardwell! We are so happy to meet you. Our boys are so excited to come to your camp. I must say, I have never seen a camp so perfectly built for total accessibility," said Josh's Dad.

"You can call me Bart," said the Director. "When I was in an accident right after college, I had to decide what to do with my life. A Christian Summer Camp was what fit me and fueled my faith as I built it."

"Now, most of my family work here or are involved in some way. Our community and volunteers have helped it to grow into this wonderful, Spiritual retreat and Renewal of Faith."

"We are very involved with helping Veterans recover and get back to as normal life as they can. So, if you know any Veterans, tell them about us."

"It has been very rewarding to watch my dream come to life. To see and become a part of people growing and becoming whole."

As everyone was given a tour around camp, there were lots of oohs and ahhs. Wherever you looked, so much love and care had gone into the buildings, the gardens, and the landscaping.

A river ran right beside the camp. The petting zoo was just down the hill from the main lodge. A zip line ran from the top of the hill, across the river, and through the woods.

Everyone was impressed. The boys were ready to try everything out, but they had to wait.

When it was time for the non-campers to leave, there was a long line of vehicles headed out the drive. Some going back home, some going on vacation, and some heading north to the Mall of America.

Nik and Josh were sharing one room. Matt and Doug were right across the hall from their friends. It was cool that each room had the name of whichever company had donated the money to build it. Nik and Josh were in the UPS Room. Matt and Doug were in the Home Depot Room.

The dining hall had tables and a few chairs. Not many chairs were needed for this week of camp. The room was filled with wheelchairs. Those who could roll and carry their trays headed to the serving area. Those who needed some help had their own helpers, or the staff stepped in to give a hand. Not everyone can balance a tray and roll their chair.

The salad bar was filled with fresh fruit and vegetables. Every salad makings that you might like was available!

The main meal was spaghetti and meatballs, green beans, and garlic bread. It smelled so good. The boys were hungry and could hardly wait for their turn.

A variety of desserts were in the glass case. Dinner was hot and delicious. Rumor had it that there would be a surprise one evening. Someone whispered, "Maybe root beer floats!"

Everyone headed straight to bed after the evening service, which was filled with fun, spirituality, and great singing.

Tomorrow, everyone had to be up early and ready to transport to Rochester for the Chariots of Fire Race.

What a way to kick off summer camp!

4

Breakfast was a rush! Everyone was rushing to roll onto wagons and into vehicles, to get to Rochester. Kick off is 9:00am for the Chariots of Fire Race. Excitement and anticipation filled the air!

Wheelchairs, walkers, and bikes were lined up, ready to go. Nik and his friends waited in anticipation. Josh had borrowed a wheelchair.

Get ready! Get set! Go!!!!!!

The wheels were rolling, and people were flying down the road. A few people were walking or running, trying to keep up. Ten miles is a long walk!

Wagons rolled along to load up anyone who got too tired. They became cheerleaders. Cheering on the ones still in the race.

Sweaty, dirty participants started arriving back at camp.

Showers were running. Some people headed to the pool to cool off. Some were just relaxing and chatting with old and new friends.

When the boys entered the Lodge to get ready for dinner, they were surprised to see tables set up. Staff members were standing or sitting by the table with the sign-up sheets for their events.

Everyone had to go around to sign up for the events they wanted to participate in. The tables were full of choices.

As the boys rolled through the tables, they were surprised at all the variety to choose from.

"Look at that!" said Nik. "I might like to try horseback riding! Do you think I could sit in the saddle? I've always loved horses."

"Wow!" Josh whispered. "I can't believe we can play golf and tennis in a wheelchair!"

Matt looked around, trying to decide what he wanted to do. "Hey, Nik! Look at this! We can play baseball and basketball! I never thought I could play again. This is so amazing!"

Doug laughed, "You guys have no idea what you can do, if you want to. When I first came here, I thought I would just sit back and kinda watch everyone do their thing. I had no intention of letting people see me try something and fail. My pride almost ruined my week at camp."

"But Bart hung out with me for a while and convinced me that it was better to live my life than to sit back and watch it pass me by. He said it was better to try and fail than to just give up and never try."

"Once I decided to try some activities, I found out that I was pretty competitive. I learned a lot about myself that first year."

"I used to let people do things for me all the time. It was easier and faster. I never made a mess or looked dumb."

"Here at camp, they don't volunteer to help you unless you ask for help. When you see people with more severe disabilities than your own, trying over and over and laughing at their mistakes, it really wakes you up. I finally decided that I needed to start growing up."

"My parents were shocked when I went home. I started making my own bed and doing chores around the house. I did so much more for myself. You guys are much more mature than I was. You are all going to have a blast!"

"Okay!" Nik said. "Tomorrow, I'm getting on a horse! I signed up for it, first thing in the morning."

Josh laughed, "Me too! If you fall off, I'll take your picture and then I'll help you up."

Nik rolled his eyes. He had almost forgotten what a joker Josh could be. But sharing this experience with his best friend was going to be so cool.

When the friends compared their lists for events, they had a few similar, but most of the offered events were covered. They figured whichever ones they didn't do this year, they'd do them next summer.

Doug explained that there were a few group events that everyone participated in, like baseball, miniature golf, water skiing, and a few others.

Nik shook his head in amazement. "How can we get these all done in one week?"

Josh laughed, "You just keep moving! You will get into a routine. At first, it seems like a lot, but we will be so busy having fun, you'll just go with the flow. I promise you can do it."

"Wow!" Matt said. "Makes me think of Football Camp, except that was all about football. At least here, there's a lot of different things. This is going to be so much fun."

"Wait until I tell Gramps what all we got to experience. He is going to be so impressed."

5

"Hey, look!" Josh shouted. "There's a gift shop! Who would have thought there would be a gift shop at summer camp?"

Nik looked over at Josh and laughed. "I bet they won't have what you usually shop for. No expensive shoes or sports equipment."

"Come on! Let's check it out. I want to take home some kind of souvenir."

The Team of four wandered through the shop looking at different things. Nik bought a cap to keep the sun out of his eyes. Matt found some odds and ends for little gifts. Doug got a water bottle, and Josh found a new sweatshirt jacket.

They all left the shop with a smile.

Everyone lined up for a group picture in front of the Lodge. "I never saw so many wheelchairs in one place," Josh said. "Maybe I can get good enough to win a race."

"It's fun to win, Josh, but sometimes just being in a group and doing your best is pretty satisfying," Matt said.

Nik rolled back and forth a couple times before he stopped by Doug.

"Doug, have you ridden a horse? I think I'm a little nervous. They are pretty high off the ground."

Doug patted Nik on the back, "Not to worry, buddy! They have it all set up, so you will be safe. They have staff right with you. Your butt will stay in the saddle just fine."

When the sun came up, Nik sat up in bed with a determined attitude. "Today is the day! Let's get moving, Josh! Breakfast is calling our name. We have to get done eating and head towards the stables."

"Gee, Nik! Why the rush? Are you afraid you'll chicken out?" Josh laughed as he reached for his cap. "Let's roll, buddy!"

As Nik and Josh headed up the hill to the stables, they could hear the horses blowing and shuffling. There were a few whinnies as the horses were moved into the stalls to wait their turn for a rider.

"Do you think we can pet them, Josh? Their noses look like velvet. I have never touched a horse before. They are big, but they seem friendly enough."

"Come on, Nik! Let's get in line, or we might miss our turn."

"Oh, wow!" Nik whispered. "Who would have thought that I could do this? I am riding a horse! Someone, please take a picture."

Doug rolled in as Nik was dismounting. "How'd you like it, Nik?"

"I love it! I think I would like to find a place to ride near home." Nik rolled out of the barn with a big smile.

Josh ran to catch up once he dismounted. "Gosh! That was pretty cool. I never rode before. Did you like it, Nik? You didn't have any problems, did you?"

"It was great, Josh! Maybe we can find somewhere to ride near home. Of course, you have Football Practice starting pretty soon."

When lunch was over, it was time for Miniature Golf. It was sweet having a course designed for wheelchairs. Nik thought it was so much better than the course at home, where he had to roll off in the grass and try to hit the balls.

Josh complained that he couldn't hit the balls through the little holes. The other boys teased him that he was just used to playing with big footballs. He didn't have a delicate touch. He was used to charging headfirst and getting clobbered.

After dinner, which was amazing, the boys wanted to go swimming. Matt couldn't stop talking about the barbecue from dinner. "I can't believe they made a giant grill from an old Steam Engine. That was the best barbecue I've had since I left St. Louis!"

Doug had to agree, "They do feed us good. Of course, we burn it off all day with all our activities. I think that tomorrow is tacos. I love tacos! But everything they cook here is so good."

Josh groaned, "I think I ate too much! I am going to run the trails for a while. I'll meet you guys at the chapel."

The boys all grabbed inner tubes and floated for a while.

"This is the perfect way to end a busy, hot day," Matt said with a sigh. "This camp makes me want to look for challenges and start having dreams again. I guess I just thought getting through each day was enough since my accident. Now, I think I'm really ready to dream and make plans."

"I may not play football, but there are other professions in the sports arena. I could coach. I could be an announcer. Endless possibilities! I have to talk with Gramps. He would know what opportunities are out there."

6

Every evening after dinner, there were games, a spiritual message, and treats.

Sometimes the message was just to make everyone stop and think. Why do I do that? What could I have done differently? Am I a person that I would want for a friend? Am I a good friend? What would make me a better person or a better friend?

Minute to Win It Games were fun to watch. Hard to do. If you don't try, you can't win! Josh had to give it a try. Watching him try to move Oreo Cookies from his eyebrow to his mouth with just using his facial muscles was hilarious. The boys laughed all the way to the Chapel. They took turns trying to copy his wild face movements.

The Chapel was a beautiful log cabin. It had a high, vaulted ceiling and amazing stained-glass windows. Nik sat there wondering if all churches were built with high ceilings and beautiful windows. Did God spend time in each one?

Did Angels come to church? Maybe that was why the music was so beautiful and made you wonder about Heaven. He could just imagine what it would sound like when all the angels sang. Did churches bring out the best in people? So many questions!

Each night, the music was great. Special speakers and singers came to share their talents. It was very exciting and different from what the boys were used to.

One man in particular impressed the boys. The man had no arms or hands. He played his guitar with his toes. He was awesome. They really loved him and his music. As much as they loved sports, that night they wished they could sing and play music like him.

Another evening brought a speaker who was a mountain climber. He had gotten trapped between two big rocks. He was alone on top of a mountain. He was going to freeze to death if he stayed there. He used his pocket knife to cut off his foot.

No one said a word. Every person was thinking, "Could I have done that?" They were all grateful that they didn't have to make that choice.

He was still a mountain climber, even with his prosthetic foot. He always had to carry a bag of extra feet and tools to work on them. Different feet were made for different surfaces. He wore out a lot of feet. Every camper who had feet looked at them and felt fortunate.

Bart, the Director, happened to have four daughters. One was a little older, and the other three were triplets. They were very pretty girls. Bart and his family sang and worked in ministry. The camp was strictly a family business.

When the girls sang, the boys were very impressed. That night, the girls were the main topic of conversation as they got ready for bed. They had so many questions about how the girls had grown up working with their Dad.

When Nik checked the schedule for tomorrow's activities, he got excited. "Yeah! Tomorrow we're playing baseball after lunch!"

"I think I might take my bike through the trails after breakfast. I saw that they have some extra bikes by the office, if you want to come."

Josh yawned and stretched. "I might or I could run the trails to stay in practice. I think I'd like to visit the little farm sometime tomorrow. I heard the Triplets are feeding the babies."

"We'll see how the schedule plays out. Good night, Josh."

Nik was awakened by the pounding on his door. "Wake up! We're going for an early morning bike ride. Come on, Nik!" Doug loved riding his bike, and he wanted Nik to join him,

"Okay! Give me a minute to get dressed. Good grief! It's only 5 o'clock! Are you guys crazy?"

"No! We just want to get as much riding in as we can. Once we go home, we never have friends to share it with, and our schedules get too busy."

"I'll be right out!" Nik called out as he pulled on a sweatshirt. "I'm pretty sure it's not warm at five in the morning. What am I doing? Oh yeah, I'm getting the most out of my week at camp. You go ahead and get your beauty rest, Josh!" Nik whispered as he rolled out the door.

7

"What took you so long?" laughed Doug. "This is the group of morning racers. Thanks for joining us!"

"Wow!" Nik rolled onto the driveway and stopped. There were about a dozen guys and a couple girls. Some were in racing chairs, and some were on bikes. They were rolling back and forth and around in circles. They were warming up before rolling out.

"Do you do his every morning?" asked Nik. "This is crazy! But let's get going. I'm too excited to sit still!"

Doug rolled beside Nik to get started. "Who are these guys?" Nik asked. "They look like weight lifters or professional athletes."

Doug laughed, "Yeah, they are all that, and they are our staff and instructors for this week. They fly in from all over the country and overseas to help Bart this week. When you are a Champion, you usually know other Champions. They get together to make this an awesome week for us. They like to say that they are training the Future champions."

"How can they be Instructors? They're all in wheelchairs."

"Nik, this camp is going to teach you so much. You will discover that Bart is a World Champion Racer, and he brings his friends to teach us how to overcome challenges and come out as champions.”

“But, Doug! One guy has no legs and rolls around on a skateboard. How can he be an Instructor?”

“You will see that a lot of these guys have overcome obstacles and are miracles in themselves. I have learned that our greatest disability is in our minds. If we tell ourselves that we can’t do something, we can’t. A positive attitude and determination will help you to achieve the impossible.”

“Get rolling, kid!” Doug took off, and Nik decided to try to keep up.

Nik decided that next time, he would forget the sweatshirt. The sun was coming up, and he noticed that every cobweb in the trees was shiny with dew. He hadn’t noticed them when everything was dry. Nik laughed as he pushed himself to keep up.

Who would have thought that waking up with the birds could be fun?

The sky was turning blue, and the birds were digging in the forest floor for bugs and worms. It was kinda cool to be there watching the world wake up.

Nik was the last one to enter the dining room. He was panting and sweaty, but he was smiling from ear to ear.

Doug called him over to join him and a couple other morning riders. "Glad to see you made it!" Doug said before introducing the others.

"It's been great meeting you guys," Nik said. "Thanks for letting me join you. I'd like to ride with you again, if that's okay?"

"Now I have to rethink what I'm going to do this morning. I don't think I have the energy left to hit the trails. Maybe I will go with Josh to watch the Triplets feed the baby animals."

Josh was in their room, packing his backpack for the day.

"Hey, man! Where you been? Did you miss breakfast?"

"Hi Josh! I need to jump in the shower, and then I will go with you to the petting farm."

"Okay, Nik! Where did you disappear to this morning? You were gone before I even woke up."

Nik started getting dressed as he told Josh about his early morning bike ride. "I had breakfast after our ride. You won't believe who our Instructors are. You are going to be really surprised."

"I watched the sun come up. I watched the forest wake up. It was really cool. Early in the morning, when everyone is sleeping, it's really quiet. I heard birds and squirrels searching for breakfast. I never even thought about where they got their food. It's really amazing how God has provided every creature with what they need."

Josh shook his head. "I can't believe you guys went without me! But thanks! I would rather sleep."

"I was planning on hitting the trails this morning, but I ran out of energy. I'll go with you to the petting farm, if you don't mind."

"Sure! We'd better get going, or the girls will have everything fed before we get there. I wonder what all they have?"

"This is a perfect day!" Nik said. "The sky is so blue and the fluffy little clouds look like they're just floating around. I'm glad it's not rainy!"

8

Nik rolled down the hill with Josh jogging beside him. They followed the road through the curves. When it straightened out, there was the little red barn with pens and cages.

They could hear all the animal sounds before they even got close. It was breakfast time, and the animals were ready to eat. Nik felt a tug at his heart. It reminded him of his Grandma's farm.

"Look at that!" said Nik as he rolled closer to the cage with a big hawk in it. "It says here that he's recuperating from an injury. We can't get too close, but I've never seen a hawk even this close. He is so big! Look at the size of his feet and those talons. I wonder how he got injured."

"Yeah! Here come the girls. Let's see what they're up to. Maybe we can give them a hand."

The boys listened as the girls explained the morning routine. They told them about the different animals. They explained why some had to be separated from the others and why some had to be bottle-fed. Nik smiled. It was just like being back at the farm.

The scents, the sounds, and the chores. He really missed spending that time with his Grandma. Great memories!

There were a couple dogs that followed the girls everywhere. Nik missed his dog, Buddy. But his Mom had said that she would take good care of him.

They saw eggs and baby chicks in the incubator. The rooster strutted and crowed like he was proud of himself.

There were baby bunnies in the hutches. The boys got to hold and feed them. They laughed as the bunnies twitched their noses and blinked their eyes. They bottle-fed some calves and lambs. The boys laughed at what messy eaters they were.

The mini goats bounced and jumped on every surface that they could reach. Their fence had to be really high. They were little acrobats. The boys fed them through the fence.

Meeting Clyde the Camel was interesting. They had never seen a real camel, only in books. He was very friendly. He was very cool. He acted like he wanted to follow them around, but he had to stay in his enclosure. He was too young to ride, but sometimes they put a blanket or rug on his back. That would make it easier to work up to a saddle someday.

"Hey, guys! It's time to head up to lunch. It's almost baseball time!"

Josh said, "Are you girls gonna play?"

"Of course!" one of the Triplets replied. "We're gonna kick your butts!"

"Let's eat on the deck," Josh suggested. "It's really nice out here, and I think we smell a little like the farm animals."

The sun was shining, but it wasn't too hot. "This is really perfect weather for playing baseball."

When the blessing was said and everyone was seated, the conversation continued. Nik asked the Triplets what they did when they weren't helping at camp.

"Sometimes we go with our family to promote camp. Sometimes we go cheer our Dad on at his races. Most of the time, we just go to school, like everyone else."

"This is the coolest camp that I have ever heard of. People come from all over the world. How do they even know about it?" asked Nik.

"We help in a lot of countries. If we hear about a need for wheelchairs, we contact groups that will help in that area. If a group or town needs medical help or a well dug or whatever, we put them in touch with groups that can help in those situations."

"One thing that our Dad put together is sending wheelchairs to Africa. We actually have some guys who come to camp from there. Can you imagine just crawling in the dirt for your whole life? People with disabilities have no help in many countries. No medical, no equipment, no support. They are either forgotten or abused. It's very rewarding to know that our little bit of help is changing lives."

"I never realized how lucky we were to live in this country," said Nik. "Maybe there's something that we could all do to make other people's lives better."

"If you look around, there's always something that you can do to help someone. My Dad said an awful lot of people just don't want to see what makes them uncomfortable."

"Time's up, boys! We girls are gonna teach you all how to play ball. Let's rock and roll! Josh, you have to grab a chair."

9

"Strike three! You're out!" shouted Bart. "Let's get some energy going here! Don't let my little girls beat you!"

"Next time, let's balance our teams better, Boss. I don't think all the girls should be on the same team," said the Tennis Instructor. "Give the boys a fair chance. Some of these guys are playing for the first time."

"Okay," said Bart. "Next time, we'll let the girls be the captains, and they can choose their team members. Okay, guys, what will they remember you for? Before this game is over, give them something to remember you for! Now, let's play some ball! No more whining!"

"Oh, my goodness!" Matt moaned. "I have never played so hard to lose a game. They were tougher than my sister!"

Nik laughed, "You tried your best. Tomorrow we'll do better. Now, we actually, kinda know how to play in our chairs. At least, we didn't fall out of our chairs and have to be picked up."

"Can you believe that not one person got embarrassed or angry? Of course, most of these guys have been friends for years. I hope we can be friends like that forever," Nik laughed. "Of course, if you fall out of your chairs, I will have to laugh before I help you up."

When Matt saw Nik looking around, he pointed to the storage shed. "If you're looking for Josh, he's helping the Triplets put away the equipment. I think he's a little fascinated by them."

Nik rolled over to tell Josh that he was going to take a shower before dinner. Josh gave him a thumbs-up and kept handing in the equipment. Nik smiled and rolled back to the lodge.

Nik was thinking about how many new friends they had made in a short time. Some, he may never see again, but he would remember them. If he could be even half as strong and fast as these guys, he would be happy. He was wondering how he could help other people.

"What's on the schedule for tomorrow?" Nik asked as he was putting on his socks and shoes. "When are we doing the zip line?"

"We could do that in the morning. We're going bowling and to the Pizza Ranch for lunch," Josh mumbled as he combed his hair.

"You know if it rains, we could play dodgeball or basketball in the gym."

Nik rolled close to Josh. "Do you have on cologne? Oh, you smell good. I'm sure the Triplets will notice. Are they singing tonight?"

"What do you think of doing the zip line after bowling?" said Josh. "That way, it won't be such a tight schedule in the morning. I heard through the grapevine that tonight, before service, we might have root beer floats."

When the boys entered the dining room, it was packed. "Oh, no!" Josh said. "I don't think we'll be able to sit together. Why do you think there are so many extra people here tonight?"

"Well," Nik replied. "Maybe tonight we'll have some special speaker or singer. Some of these people are really dressed up and look important."

Matt waved Nik over to sit with him. Josh sat nearby with a new friend. "Have you seen her yet? I heard that Miss wheelchair USA is here."

Nik looked at Matt and smiled. "Do you know who she is? I saw a new, glittery pink bike out front. Do you think she might stay at camp and ride with us?"

"It's been kept a secret, I guess," said Matt. "It would be pretty cool to meet a Queen and maybe tell people that I went riding with a Queen at dawn."

Dinner that evening was roast beef and mashed potatoes with strawberry shortcake. Everyone ate and helped clean up, so no one would be late for the special speaker. Bart announced that root beer floats would be served after service tonight.

Clouds were rolling across the sky as everyone headed to the Chapel. Distant thunder was rumbling. Matt said, "Maybe it will pass through quickly. Maybe the storm will take away some of the heat and mosquitoes."

"You know it's summertime," Nik said. "We have to have a little rain and bugs."

"Do you think we can still do the zip line if it rains?" Josh asked. "Maybe since we're doing the zip line in the afternoon, it won't matter."

Nik laughed. "It won't matter. If we can't do it tomorrow, we'll do it the next day."

Rain started falling just as they entered the Chapel. Candles were lit and flickering. Music was playing softly. Everyone seemed to sense that this was a special event. Everyone sat quietly waiting for something special.

10

When the Chapel doors closed, the boys noticed that there were cameras everywhere. This was certainly a special night.

Bart opened the service with a message about looking inside yourself to see how far you have come. What have you learned this week? How have you grown?

"Everyone comes to camp to have fun and meet new friends," Bart said. "Every day of our lives, we make choices, small and large. Every person that we meet teaches us something."

"Not one of you will go home exactly as you were when you arrived here. My purpose with this camp is to open your minds and hearts to all the possibilities that will help you to grow and mature into whole people. Even in a wheelchair, you have opportunities to do great things."

"Some of you have been to camp many times. This is the first time for some. When you newbies arrived, did you think you could do all the things that we offered? Tonight, we have a special guest. She has overcome all types of challenges. She has overcome the fear of speaking to crowds. She has learned to roll her wheelchair in an evening gown."

"Our guest tonight started coming to camp when she was a little girl. She was afraid of every activity, but pushed herself to overcome those fears. She has graced our camp many times. We have watched her grow into an amazing, confident young woman. Please welcome our newly crowned, Miss Wheelchair USA!"

All eyes watched as a very beautiful, confident young lady rolled onto the stage in a sparkling, pink wheelchair. She wore a crown and a satin sash, showing that she was a Queen in an evening gown.

"Wow!" Josh whispered. "I had no idea that we'd meet a Queen at camp."

Matt watched as the Queen rolled across the stage. "I think I'm in love! Wake me up when this is over, because this must be a dream!"

Doug smacked Nik on the shoulder and laughed. "You would think these guys had never seen a pretty girl before."

Nik shook his head and grinned. "You know we have some pretty girls at home. Reni is the prettiest. But they aren't Queens wearing a crown and sash. They don't have sparkling wheelchairs or bikes."

Miss Wheelchair USA looked out over the crowd. "This place is one of the reasons that I was crowned. I learned so much here. My confidence, my strength, my ability to choose what I wanted to do. So many of us, when we are born with a disability or become disabled, think that we have to let our disability rule our world."

"But, let me tell you a fact of life. Each day when we wake up, we have a new opportunity to create our own happy day, by the choices we make. We must look at opportunities, instead of obstacles or challenges."

"Most of us will always need some help. But look at every situation and do as much as you can for yourself. If you need help, ask for it."

"We have people who love us, and they are here to help. But don't sell yourself short. You are much more than you think you are. You are more than your walker or your wheelchair. You are all Champions in Training. I expect great things from you. Use your brain and your heart. Make your dreams come true!"

Applause filled the Chapel as she rolled off the stage. Every person at camp was impressed and encouraged.

Even while enjoying their root beer floats, the boys were quieter than usual. Knowing that someone as special as Miss Wheelchair USA cared enough about them to cheer them on and wanted the best for them made the boys look at themselves with a new awareness of what their possibilities could be.

The clouds had cleared, and the boys enjoyed sitting out in the fresh air for a while before heading to bed.

"You know, guys," said Nik. "We have to do something special! Our lives are just starting. We need to make a mark, so the world will know we existed."

All the boys dreamed of climbing mountains and slaying dragons. All the girls dreamed of being princesses. They all wanted to be Champions and do the impossible!

11

Early the next morning, Josh woke up, all excited to go biking with the morning racers. Mainly, because he would be riding with the Queen.

Nik yawned and rolled over. "I think I'll save my energy to go riding horses today. You go have some fun. I'll see you at breakfast."

Nik said over his shoulder, "Don't forget, tomorrow we'll be going water skiing and picnicking. I'm pretty excited, but a little nervous. What great experiences we are having!"

Josh laughed as he headed out the door. He ran to grab a bike and catch up with the morning riders. He could see the sparkling bike up ahead.

When Josh arrived back at the dining room for breakfast, he was out of breath. He grabbed a tray and walked over to join Nik and Doug.

"Why didn't you tell me those guys ride like beasts. I had a heck of a time keeping up. I thought I was in pretty good shape, but I think I better work a lot harder."

Nik and Doug laughed. Matt rolled up with his tray. "May I join you guys? I think I might try riding with you today, Nik. I've decided to try some new things. I want to get more rounded in my activities. Football and basketball have really been my life. I think I need to expand my horizons."

"Sure!" Josh said. "I heard Miss Wheelchair USA say that she was riding this morning. I hope they have enough horses. I think quite a few guys are headed to the stables this morning."

Nik laughed. "Maybe I'll go work in the garden this morning. The Landscaper was telling me that a shipment of flowers had been delivered. I think I might like getting down in the dirt for a while."

Josh looked at Nik like he was crazy. "You came to a sports camp to have fun. Why do you want to work?"

Nik smiled at his best friend. "Josh, I enjoy planting and working in the garden. I've always helped my Mom and Grandma plant and weed. It gives me a chance to get out of my chair, and it feels good."

"Well, my friend," Josh said as he put his tray away. "Have fun playing in the dirt. I'm going to see what else is going on."

When Nik got outside, he decided to roll around a little while to see what camp was really like, without a crowd.

He rolled up to the cooks' cabin and noticed some weeds in the flower bed. He scooted forward and eased down to the ground.

He found a bucket sitting near the front door. He was humming as he pulled weeds out of the ground and dropped them in the bucket.

He was just finishing when Bart drove by in his Gator. Bart backed up and sat watching Nik. "What in the world are you doing, Nik? Have you really run out of things to do with your friends?”

Nik laughed, “I wanted to get out of my chair for a while and do some gardening. I wanted to leave some kind of mark here at camp.”

“Well, if you really want to leave a mark, would you like to do some painting? We’re trying to freshen up the gym. Go tell the guys that you want to help. They will appreciate your help.”

“Thanks, Bart! This is great! I’m on my way, as soon as I wash my hands.”

Nik could smell the paint before he even got to the gym. He rolled in smiling. “Hey, guys! Bart said I could lend a hand. Got an extra brush?”

The guys on staff looked at Nik. “Hey, kid, did you run out of fun stuff to do? Nobody offers to work at camp!”

Nik shook his head. “Sometimes I need to do something that makes me feel like I did something to help someone else. I think I like being useful and making the camp better, makes me feel good.”

The painting crew laughed. “Knock yourself out, kid. We appreciate your help. It feels like we’ve been painting all summer.”

“No, Tracy!” one of the guys said. “We’ve only been painting this week. It just feels like all summer.”

"You guys are so lucky to have such a great camp to work at," said Nik. "Do you get to try all the different activities when you're not working?"

"Yeah!" Tracy said. "It is a pretty cool place to work. Bart is great to work for. We keep trying to beat him and his friends at different events. Those guys are like Superman. They can overcome and achieve anything."

"I guess when you are World Champions, you just get used to winning," Nik said. "I better get done. I have to meet my friends for lunch."

12

The boys were up before the sun. They were excited about going water skiing. Breakfast was eaten, and everyone was ready to load up in vans to head to the river.

When they arrived, it was a sunny, breezy day. Little fluffy clouds floated across the sky. A shelter house had been set up for lunchtime. Brats and hot dogs were ready to go on the grills.

The sun made the water ripples shine like twinkling diamonds. It was the perfect day to play in the water.

"Wow!" said Josh. "I smell the brats and hot dogs. I can hardly wait until lunch."

Matt laughed. "Josh, you are always hungry! Let's check out what's happening by the water."

"Look at that!" said Nik. "We can try anything we want. There's pontoons, motorboats, and skis. There's also kayaks and jet skis. Where shall we start?"

Matt decided to check out the jet skis first. Doug went over to see how everyone would be set up to water ski.

Nik watched all the activity. "Hey, Josh! Have you ever water-skied before? I think I would like to try the kayak first. What do you think?"

Josh looked around. "Maybe I'll try the kayak first with you. And then we could go for a ride on one of the pontoons."

"We could wait until after lunch to water ski," Nik thought out loud. "We can watch to see how everyone else does first."

Tom was in charge of the kayaks. He made sure everyone wore a life vest and learned how to handle the kayak before he let go. Josh and Nik tipped out a couple times before they got the hang of it.

They were laughing and shaking water out of their eyes by the time they could paddle in a circle and then away from the shore.

They watched all the other campers laughing and having fun.

"I think everyone's having a lot of fun water skiing," said Nik. "I think after lunch, I'll be ready. How about you, Josh? Here comes the pontoon. Let's get over to the loading dock."

"This is so cool!" Nik sighed. Sitting back, letting the wind dry his hair, and watching the scenery fly by. "I think my Dad should get one of these."

Josh laughed, "We better just enjoy our adventures here. This is not our real world. This is like a fantasy land. We don't even have a big body of water by us!"

Grilled hot dogs and brats were served with baked beans and chips under the shelter house. When everyone had eaten and relaxed, it was back to the water.

"Okay!" said Nik. "Let's do this! You only live once. If everyone else can water ski, so can I. Gee, even the little kids are skiing."

The motorboat pulled the floating seat off the dock. With a surprised squeak, Nik was flying through the water. In the excitement of the moment, out in the middle of the river, Nik let go of the rope handles.

At first, he started to panic, but then he realized he was just floating in the water. Everyone cheered as the boat circled around to pick him back up.

When he got near the shore, he let go, like he was supposed to. Then, he just floated to the beach. When he landed, some of the staff put him back into his chair. He sat and watched his friends ski and then float back to shore.

"Wow! What a day!" Matt said. "This has got to be the best day of my life! When we go home, it's going to be a real let-down."

"Maybe not," Nik replied. "I have an idea. I'll share it later."

The trip back to camp was pretty quiet. Almost everyone was a little or a lot sunburned. Some napped and some chatted quietly.

All the campers were packed and ready to head home. Some had families coming to pick them up. Some had to be delivered to the bus station or the airport.

Lots of hugs and phone numbers were exchanged as everyone rolled out.

"Well, boys!" Matt's Dad asked. "Was it as great as you thought it would be?"

Matt looked tired, but he was smiling. "It went beyond our expectations! We have some new ideas."

"Oh, no!" Josh's Dad groaned. "I thought you guys might be so exhausted that you might want to coast for a little while."

"Oh, Dad!" Josh laughed. "We are never that tired."

The boys told their parents about the camp activities and then slept all the way home.

13

Nik decided to be a little lazy and hang out around the house. His Mom was working on a special project in her workshop. The house was quiet.

Buddy was pacing, so Nik took him out for a walk and then played under the water sprinklers. He was thinking about how lucky he was.

He had never had to crawl through the dirt or beg for anything. His family had made sure his needs were met, and he was loved unconditionally. His big brothers taught him so much and included him in their special activities.

Nik felt very fortunate, and he decided to make sure his family knew how much they meant to him. Buddy followed him into the house.

Mom was cleaning her hands and arms. "What are you up to, my young man? You look like you're very deep in thought."

"Hi, Mom! When Dad gets home, can we sit down and spend some time together? I feel like I need some time with you guys."

Nik met his Dad at the door when he came home from work.

"To what do I owe this honor?" Dad said as he hung up his jacket and hat. "You don't usually meet me at the door unless you need something, Nik. What can I do for you?"

"We have been so busy that we haven't got to do anything just for us lately," Nik said. "If you're not busy tomorrow, can we go fishing? Mom said she would make a picnic lunch. I would like to spend the day with my favorite people in the whole world. We could let Buddy run for a little bit."

"You are right, son. We need our time together. It's great to have friends and help other people. But we need our family time, too. Do you want to invite any of your friends?"

"Not this time, Dad! Just our little family."

"I'll get our fishing gear ready, and we can leave after breakfast tomorrow. I think Buddy needs some running time. He has spent most of the summer in the house. Make sure to wear your fishing hat. You don't want to get a sunburn."

"Okay, Dad! Thanks for worrying about me. I think Mom baked some chocolate chip cookies. Maybe she'll pack some. I'll put some bottles of water in the fridge to get cold. We always get thirsty when we're fishing."

"Hey, Dad!" Nik said. "Can I use the new, blue rod with the open reel? I promise I will try not to tangle it up again. I like how light it is."

"Sure, Nik! You can't get good at something if you don't practice. I'm sorry I got irritated last time. It wasn't really about the tangled line. I brought my irritation home from work and accidentally took it out on you. I try not to do that. I will try harder."

"It's okay, Dad! Sometimes, I get frustrated, too. I go out and knock the tetherball around. You could do that when you have a bad day."

"Nik, you are good for my soul! You humble me with your open heart. Mom and I are so fortunate to have you in our lives. We never know what you will say or do. You bring out the best in us."

"Dad, something at camp really touched my heart. Did you know that there are countries where they have no services or equipment for people with disabilities? I am so grateful that I don't have to crawl in the dirt."

"You are right, Nik. Our country has created a wonderful system to help families with special needs. We have agencies to help with almost anything."

"If you had been born a hundred years ago, first, you wouldn't have survived. They didn't have the medical knowledge to repair broken hearts. And, if by some miracle, you had survived, you couldn't have gone to school or had your cool equipment."

"They didn't have racing bikes or bathtub lifts or ramps to get in and out of the house. I am so happy that we can help you grow up to become whatever you want to be. Many people, even without disabilities, don't have the love and support that you have."

"I know, Dad! That's why I want to help other people. I know how lucky I am. Mostly, because of you and Mom. I love you guys for all you do for me. Dad, do you remember what Bart, at camp, told us? He wanted to do something to help other people. He has changed lives in so many ways. I want to be just like him. I want to help people grow and be whole. Do you think I can do something like that?"

Dad shook his head. "Kid, you always amaze me! I think that whatever you set your mind to do, you will make it happen. Enough deep thinking! Let's go fishing. Mom and Buddy are in the van."

"Let's go! The fish are calling our names." Nik laughed, "I am going to catch the biggest fish. I feel lucky today!"

Mom spread a blanket on the ground as the guys got their equipment set up. Buddy was running in circles, trying to catch a butterfly. A rabbit hopped out from under a bush, so Buddy changed directions to chase the rabbit. The rabbit went under a pile of logs and out of sight.

"Come back, Buddy!" Mom called. "Leave the bunny alone. Here's a bone. Why don't you relax here with me for a few minutes, while the guys catch some fish?"

The sun was shining, and the light breeze felt just right. The scent of honeysuckle was in the air. It was a perfect day to do nothing but relax and enjoy family time.

When Buddy decided to chase a bumblebee, Mom called him back. "You don't want to get your nose stung, Buddy. Let's get lunch ready. The guys will be up here soon, and they will be hungry."

Dad was pushing Nik's chair up the hill. Nik had the stringer of fish.

"Look, Mom! Can we have these for dinner tonight?"

"You might need a few more for dinner," Mom laughed. "Put those in the bucket of cold water. We'll put them in the cooler when we head home."

"I think it would be a good idea to clean them before we leave here. I am happy to cook them for you, but I don't clean fish."

Dad laughed. "Don't worry, Mama. We men will do the dirty work."

"Let me get Nik back to fishing, and I will be right back."

Buddy followed them down to the water. He was happy to sit with Nik.

Dad sat with Mom, relaxing and watching Nik and Buddy.

"In a couple more years, we'll have to start checking out colleges. Has Nik talked about what he might like to do? Has he mentioned any particular school?"

"Remember when he was little?" Mom asked. "First, they said he might not live to see his first birthday. Then they said he probably wouldn't live past his teens. Now, he's healthier than ever, and we're talking about college. I think he has surprised all his doctors. Of course, it's because he's stubborn and bull-headed like his Dad!"

"Remember when he was little and afraid of everything?" Dad laughed. "He was afraid of bugs, worms, and fish. His brothers kept him screaming with their teasing. Our picnics are certainly calmer now."

"Yes," Mom said. "But, we had so much fun with our boys. I miss those crazy days. You should call the other boys and ask them to come fishing with us. I bet they miss our crazy days, too. I'm sure the Grandkids would have fun, even if they just run and chase the butterflies with Buddy."

Dad stood up and stretched. "I'll call them when we get home. Right now, I gotta get back to fishing, before Nik catches all my fish."

Just as Dad reached the bank, Buddy jumped into the water trying to help Nik reel in a big fish.

"I can't leave you two alone for five minutes," Dad laughed. "Buddy, get out of there! Let me help you, Nik. I have the net. Oh, good grief, Buddy, could you walk away to shake off your water?"

Nik laughed so hard that his chair almost tipped over. "Do you think we have enough for dinner?"

Dad shook his head. "You guys are stinkers! First, you catch my big fish, and then you get me all wet!"

"Sorry, Dad! Are we done yet? We need to clean these fish so we can go cook them. I can hardly wait to eat fried fish and fresh vegetables from our garden. Everything tastes better when we've grown it or caught it."

"Okay," Dad said. "We have plenty of fish. Let's get to work!"

14

Getting caught up with the Paper Shredding Business kept the boys busy for a few days. Nik enjoyed playing with Buddy and rolling around the neighborhood. By the second week home, Nik was ready to share his ideas with his friends.

After Matt and Josh were settled on the deck with cool drinks, Nik started talking.

"You know, guys! There's no reason that we can't have our own little Sports Club right here at home. We know most of the kids in Special Olympics. I know some won't want to join, but I think we could get enough to have some fun."

"Just think how much stronger and faster they would be if we had ongoing events or little competitions."

"Maybe we could get some of the regular athletes to help. It would help them and the Special Olympians."

Josh looked a little doubtful.

"Come on, Josh! Remember how much fun we had at Special Olympics? We could have weekly club meetings."

Matt was listening and thinking. "Should we get my Grandfather's input? There might be things we need to know before we jump into this."

"Sure!" Nik nodded. "We want everyone to have fun and be safe. I was thinking, we could call our club 'The Knight's Quest'. We could make a schedule and set goals."

"We could have different groups within the club, like the Road Racers, the Muscle Men, and the Speed Devils. This could be really fun. Some of these kids will never get to attend a cool camp. Let's use our experiences to give them something special."

Matt's Grandfather watched the boys roll up on his deck. He laid his newspaper down on the table beside his coffee cup and reading glasses.

"Hello, gentlemen! What do you have on your minds? It looks like you're on a mission."

"Gramps, we have an idea to start a sports club. We want to work on different sports and have little competitions. Like, once a week we'd get together and have fun, but also work on skills. Is there anything that we should be aware of or be worried about?"

"Well, guys, I think having adult involvement is important. I also think having your meetings at a secure place, like the school, might be best. They would have insurance, just in case someone got hurt. So, if you're serious about this, let me see what rules and guidelines the school might have."

"Gee, Gramps, you are the best! I knew you'd know what to do."

"You boys are something else! I'm really proud of you all."

The boys sat there thinking and planning, while Gramps made some phone calls.

Nik said, "If we can do this, we should get t-shirts made with our club name on them. We could have a picture of a knight's shield with our club name on it. Wouldn't it be cool to have a group of us in our Knights' quest t-shirts racing down the street or around the track?"

"Okay, boys!" Gramps said. "We need to get your parents together and set up a meeting at school. They want to know details about your club. I will sign up as your coach."

"Grandpa, you are my Superman! I don't know what we would do without you."

"Okay, my friends," said Nik. "We have a mission. Matt, do you think Reni might like to make up some posters for us? See if she might like to be in our club. I'm sure we'll have other girls join. She has some great skills to share."

Matt smiled. "I'm pretty sure she will want to be a part of this adventure. She was kinda disappointed that she couldn't go to Sports Camp. Next year, she might tag along. I'm sure she would love it. I think we should let Bart's slogan be ours. Don't Quit! Finish Strong! He will forever be my role model."

Nik smiled. "Tomorrow will be a new day, and I am excited!"

15

Matt, Nik, Josh, and Doug, along with their parents, sat in the conference room at the High School. The School Board Members sat across the table, asking questions.

"Can you tell us what your plans are? Why should we let you set up a club here at our school? Will this help in our education plans? Please give us some details."

Nik was the first to speak. "We four, Matt, Josh, Doug, and myself went to a special sports camp this summer. We learned so much and had so much fun. We want to share what we have learned."

Matt raised his hand. "We discovered that we could do so much more than we thought we could. We want to continue growing and share it with other kids. Some may never have the opportunity to attend a camp like that, but we can share what we have learned."

Josh spoke up. "I have learned so much about myself and how to help others. I learned how to adapt so many things to make sure all the kids can participate in activities. I used to think handicapped people couldn't do things. Now, I know there's not much they can't do."

Doug raised his hand. "I have been going to Ironwood Springs Sports Camp for a few years. I know people with no legs, blind, quadraplegics, deaf. It doesn't matter. With the right adaptations and support, we can all set goals. We can have dreams. Together, we can work to make them all come true."

Matt's Grandfather stood up. "Ladies and gentlemen. This is a new idea here. But, as a retired coach and a person involved with life's challenges, I would like to volunteer to be their head coach for this club, The Knight's Quest/the Achievers and Believers."

After a quiet discussion, the Board President came to sit with the families.

"All right! We have decided to give your club a trial run. We will see how much interest your group gets and how it's all run. In three months, we will meet again and you can give us a full report of how many want to join and what you are doing as a group. We need to know there's adult involvement and that you can do this safely. Good luck, gentlemen!"

After leaving the school, the families met at Nik's house.

"Oh man!" Nik laughed, "We did it! You guys are great! We need to start promoting right away. We only have three months to get organized and running!"

"Not a problem," Josh said. "I will call the radio station to invite families with special needs kids to come check us out."

"Reni has posters ready," Matt said, holding one up. "We just have to put the date, time, and place at the bottom."

Mr. Peterson smiled. "It is going to be a pleasure working with such organized and industrious young people."

"We can use the equipment in the gym and the track when it's not busy. Let's lay out our plan for our first meeting."

Nik's Mom suggested that the mothers should provide treats. She volunteered to bring cookies and bottled water for the first meeting. Each mother took a week. So the first month was covered.

Reni knocked on the door.

"Hey! I'm glad you could make it!" Nik said with a big smile. "We got approved for a trial run. We have three months to show how important our club can be to the challenged, but also to our school."

Reni laughed, "Nik, your excitement is contagious. I have a list of all the activities that I can do with the girls. This is going to be so much fun!"

When everyone had gone home, Nik called Josh to see if he wanted to go to the track.

Nik rolled over to meet Josh. "Man, I am so excited. Let's burn up some energy!"

The sun beat down on the track as the boys practiced their laps.

"Josh, don't you get tired of running all the time?" Nik asked. "Why don't we bring our bikes tomorrow? I feel like I need more speed."

"That sounds like a good idea," Josh said as he dried his face with his tank top. "I think we need a nice, cool drink. Do you think your Mom will mind if I hang out at your house for a while? If I go home, I have to mow the yard. I want to just relax a little while. When it gets a little cooler, I'll mow."

"When the sun goes down would be a good time to mow," Nik said. "My Mom is working in her workshop. We won't bother her. We have a new sprinkler system that swings around and back and forth. It's a great way to cool off. Buddy loves playing in the spray. Let's bring him out with us."

When Josh and Nik opened the door, Buddy danced all around them. As soon as they had their drinks, they headed outside. They set their drinks on the table and followed Buddy to the Sprinklers. They were laughing as Buddy ran around and around, in and out of the spray.

"Man, this feels great!" Josh laughed. "It's been ages since I enjoyed the sprinklers like this. Maybe I can talk my Dad into getting one. By the end of summer, the grass looks half dead. This is awesome!"

When the boys went on the deck to sit and have their cool lemonade, Buddy followed. He was ready to rest, too. He lapped up his from his big bowl and lay down next to Nik.

"This has been a great way to end the day," Josh said. "But, I gotta get home now. I wanna get the grass mowed before my Dad gets home. This has been a fun way to cool off. Thanks, buddy!"

Buddy looked up to see if they were talking to him. When they didn't talk to him, he went back to sleep.

"Mom!" Nik called, as he and Buddy went through the kitchen. "What's for dinner? Buddy and I are starving!"

16

"Our first meeting is Monday after school," said Matt. "I wish we knew how many kids might show up."

Mr. Peterson patted Matt on his shoulder. "Don't worry. I know there's a lot of interest in this new group."

Josh ran up the driveway, dribbling his basketball. "Hey guys! I think I can help with whoever wants to play basketball. I've been practicing with my Dad."

Matt rolled over to catch the ball. "I think we have enough experience between all of us and Gramps to cover most sports. We could occasionally invite someone special to come teach a special skill. I know a few pros who like to go coach kids. That would be something special for the kids."

Nik came racing down the street on his new red bike. "Wow!" He laughed as he rolled up on the deck. "That feels awesome! I love feeling the wind in my face."

Matt rolled over to check out Nik's bike. "I might have to get a bike, too. I know I really enjoyed the bike at camp. It was totally different from racing my chair."

"Oh yeah!" Nik smiled. "I think the only thing that I've enjoyed more was riding a horse at camp. Once we get our club running, I'm checking out Brave Hearts and Pegasus. I've been reading about them and I want to go for Riding Therapy. But, that's for another day."

"Okay, boys! What are we doing for our first meeting?"

Mr. Peterson set up his whiteboard. "We will have a mix of ages and abilities. We should probably keep it simple with a Meet and Greet."

Josh put his basketball down and sat in a red recliner. "I think we should have name tags until we get to know each other. Should we divide up by ages, abilities, or whatever sport they want to participate in?"

"Good thinking, Josh," Mr. Peterson said. "I don't think we should do every sport to start out. We need to know what each person does at Special Olympics, if they are participants."

Nik held up a paper with a few names on it. "These guys told me they're coming. Mom is bringing treats. We can't eat in the gym, but we can eat out on the patio."

"Thanks!" Mr. Peterson grinned. "I'm glad you won't make more work for me."

"By the way, guys!" Nik said with a smile. "I think we should have a knight's shield on our t-shirts. I was thinking that each time we accomplish a new sport or win a contest, we could put a patch on our shield."

"I was looking on the internet, and we can get patches really cheap for all the different sports."

Matt thought about it for a few minutes. "That's a great idea, and we could have a few special patches for when someone overcomes a fear and accomplishes something really hard."

Josh got caught up in the excitement. "We could have a code of conduct, like the real knights did. It could be: 'Be honorable, Brave, and Do Service for others.'"

Mr. Peterson was writing everything on the whiteboard. "Boys, I think this is really going to help all those kids who think they can't do things. You boys will be terrific role models and leaders. I am proud of all of you!"

17

At church on Sunday, the minister announced to the congregation that Nik and his friends were starting a club for kids with Special Needs. He gave a Blessing for their success and told everyone to tell anyone who might benefit by joining to come check it out.

Monday turned out to be chilly and rainy. As the boys sat in the gym, they worried that no one might come. When the clock struck 6:00pm, people started arriving.

About a dozen families sat on or near the bleachers. Reni sat near the doorway, making name tags. The guys were *Sir Knights* and the girls were *Ladies*.

Nik knew most of the kids from Special Olympics. It was a small group, but he was pretty sure that more would come when they got active and having fun.

Matt, Josh, and Nik welcomed everyone to their first meeting for the Ladies and Knights' Quest club.

One of the parents asked, "Exactly what kind of club is this? I see all different abilities here. What are your plans?"

Mr. Peterson stood up and introduced himself. "I think these young men have come up with a great idea. It will be fun, and it will give all the kids challenges and accomplishments. They can overcome fears, build skills in different sports, and belong to a group that will turn into best friends."

Nik rolled over by Mr. Peterson. "I think most of you know Mr. Peterson. Did you know that he is a retired coach? He has agreed to be our Club Coach. Also, all parents and Grandparents are invited to get involved and have fun with us. Maybe, if you get good enough, we'll set up a competition between the kids and the adults."

"We do want to get t-shirts made. It will cost nothing to join our club. But you need to pay for your t-shirts and take turns bringing treats. I don't want to burn my Mom out. But, thank you for getting us started."

Matt made a chart for each of the sports that the kids wanted to try. Then, one by one, he listed the names of those who wanted to try each one.

Mr. Peterson looked at the lists and congratulated the kids for being adventurous. "Today, we are getting to know each other. Next Monday, we will start our Quests. Come prepared to do your best and have fun."

When Nik rolled into church, the Minister met him at the door. He smiled and congratulated Nik on his plans for the club. "As a matter of fact," he informed Nik. "My Grandson will be coming Monday evening to check out your club. My son and his wife are pretty excited to know there's opportunities for him."

"I will be coming along to see how things are going. I am pretty excited, too! Maybe I can help out in some way. It could be a wonderful way for me to be involved with my Grandson."

"Wow!" Nik said. "We are going to have so much fun! I think this club could change people's lives. Thank you for your support. I'm sure your Grandson will love having you there."

"Mom! Dad!" Nik called as he rolled into the kitchen. "Can you believe that our Minister wants to help at our club? I think that he just wants to spend some time with his Grandson. But, that's okay!"

"I think we're getting our t-shirts tomorrow. Mr. Peterson is picking them up before the meeting." Nik rolled back and forth because he couldn't sit still. "I think I'll ride my bike around the track after lunch. I have too much energy. Maybe Josh will join me."

After Nik helped to clean off the table, he headed out the door. Josh hopped over the porch railing just as Nik rolled out. "What's up, doc?" Josh yelled as he landed. "I just talked to Matt. We're meeting at the track for a few laps."

"That's funny!" Nik said as he rolled down the ramp. "That's where I'm going, too. I need to burn up some energy. I'm so excited that I can't sit still."

Josh laughed as he ran to keep up. "Nik, I think your bike gives you wings. I'm really working hard to keep up."

Matt and Doug were at the track warming up. "Wow!" Josh gasped. "I might have to bring my bike over to keep up with you guys. Just running is too hard to keep up."

Matt laughed, "It's about time that we can do something that makes us feel like winners. We have to be role models as the Club Leaders."

Josh looked at his friends with pride. "You guys are true Champions! Everyone will love you and want to follow you anywhere."

"Hey, Doug!" Nik said. "Would you like to bring your camp video for the club to watch as we get organized tomorrow night? I think that may help them understand more about what we are trying to accomplish."

"Sure! I want these kids to want to overcome and be achievers. I'll see you guys tomorrow," Doug yelled as he rode towards home.

18

Mr. Peterson handed out the t-shirts. On the front was a picture of a knight's shield, with the name of the club, *Knights' Quest*, printed across the front. Each shirt had a name above the shield.

Nik looked at his shirt and smiled. "It's exactly as I pictured it. I love the 'Sir Nik' and all the other 'Sirs' and 'Ladies.'"

Mr. Peterson held up another stack of shirts. "These are for any parent or grandparent who wants to have some fun."

The kids' shirts were red, and the adults had blue shirts. Once everyone got their shirts on, Nik called the meeting to order. He introduced Doug, and Doug shared his camp video. After the video, there were a lot of questions from kids and adults.

Mr. Peterson raised his hand for silence. "Folks, that was for inspiration! We can't do all those activities, but we can try a lot of them. Some of those people are World Champions. We are helping the next generation of Champions right here. Are you ready to do your best, Ladies and Gentlemen?"

Nik asked, "Who wants to race your wheelchair around the track? And, if you aren't in a wheelchair, you can walk or run. Let's burn some energy!"

Nik's parents sat on a low cement wall, sipping their lemonade. "What a great group this has turned out to be!" Nik's Dad said. "These kids really put their hearts into everything they do."

Nik's Mom smiled. "These families need this fun and support. I don't think any of them ever expected their kids to have dreams and adventures. Nik's excitement for life makes us all want more."

Doug's Mom said, "I know we are all going to benefit from working together. I think Special Olympics is going to be very surprised with these athletes in a couple months."

"Okay!" Mr. Peterson called out. "Let's clean up and move out. You all did an excellent job today. I think next week we should have a little competition. Get lots of practice this week!"

Reni and Matt sat at the end of the track talking. "What do you think Gramps is planning?" Reni asked. Her ponytail was halfway down, so she pulled the clip out to let it fall around her shoulders.

"I don't know," said Matt between sips of his Gatorade. "Maybe to just get an idea of their skills and competitiveness. I know he ordered some little patches and awards. He's almost as excited as Nik."

"You know," Reni said. "I don't see you using your power chair much anymore."

Matt replied, "I really like using my muscles and strength to get around. I didn't think I would ever be able to be active and achieve things again. I am so grateful for Nik's inspiration and energy. I'm not sure I would be doing all this without his charge-ahead spirit."

"He is something, isn't he?" Reni laughed. "He brings out the best in all of us. I am really glad that we moved here. We needed a Nik in all our lives. He really brought you and Gramps back to life. I was really worried about you both."

When Nik and his parents got home, Buddy was dancing, waiting to go out. "Come on, boy! I have just enough energy to take you around the block."

Mom and Dad smiled. "I think Nik and Buddy were made for each other," said Dad. "They are both so full of energy and ready for adventures. I don't think his older brothers kept us so busy and on the go. Of course, they were pretty independent and didn't need us as much."

"I know it's different now," Mom said. "But, this is a new chapter in our lives. One of these days, Nik will be more independent. He won't always need us this much. I think I will miss the excitement."

The boys had decided that on Mondays, they would wear their club shirts to school to promote their club. They invited everyone they talked to, to come watch the competitions.

Nik was excited because some of the regular sports guys said they would be happy to help coach and time the competitions. Mr. Peterson was setting up the track equipment when a group of boys walked over to ask what they could do to help.

"Boy, oh, boy!" Josh said when he saw so many people getting involved. "I think this is really going to get a lot of attention!"

"Yes," Nik said with a grin. "I think our club is getting a lot of attention. But I think having all this support will make our special athletes and their families feel like people care about them. Our school has to be one of the best around. No other school, that I know of, has something this cool."

"I know," said Josh. "Maybe we can start something that others will want to imitate. Every kid deserves a chance to be better and stronger. I think our guys are gonna be role models for other kids and schools."

19

Mr. Peterson watched as families with athletes arrived. All the kids who had ordered shirts had them on. They rushed over to join their friends. You could tell from the parents' smiles that seeing their kids with friends made them happy. Just knowing they were accomplishing new skills and that they were happy made the parents feel that they were doing the right thing.

A good-sized crowd had come to see what the new Club was about. Reni displayed the chart that showed that today would have competitions in Running, Wheelchair Racing, and Softball Throws.

Excitement and nerves had everyone talking and guessing about who would be in each event and who might win. Bright ribbons hung on a display board, waiting to be awarded. Today, there would only be one winner in each competition.

Reni lined up everyone participating in the softball throw. Four girls and five boys were warming up their throwing arms. After each throw, a volunteer ran out to measure the distance to where the ball had landed. Each time the crowd cheered. When the last ball had been thrown, the winner went to stand or sit near Mr. Peterson.

Next came the running race. Six boys and two girls decided to compete. After lining up on the starting line, every runner waited for the whistle to blow.

When the whistle blew, they all went forward at their own pace. Two boys took off, leaving everyone else behind. One stumbled and fell. The boy behind him stopped to help his friend back up. Two boys shot ahead of them. The last of the group ran together to the finish line.

They were all cheered on. They were all winners, but only the fastest would get the ribbon.

At last, it was time for the wheelchair Race. Six chairs lined up. They were all laughing and yelling to each other to roll faster. One boy turned around to roll faster, using his foot to help push himself. Nik had to laugh because he could remember doing that when he was younger.

A couple were rolling pretty fast, one was trying to use his feet to keep going, and a couple in the back were just trying to stay in their lanes. The winner rolled over to join the other winners, waiting for their ribbons.

"Okay, folks," Mr. Peterson announced. "Today was our first competition. We will have one per month. At our weekly meetings, we will be practicing and doing some community service projects. Today's winners will receive a ribbon and their first patch to put on their shield."

"This is not a club to come watch other people do things. We are the *Believers* and *Achievers*. When we get together, we will have fun, we will build skills, and we will do our best at all times. If anyone wants to join this Club, go over there to sign up. The only thing you have to pay for is your t-shirt."

Nik and his friends agreed to meet at the track after dinner that evening.

"Yeah!" Nik cheered. "Matt got his new bike! I love it! Now we can race on the track."

"Yes," Matt laughed. "I thought I would show it to you on the way to the track. Since we're all wearing our Club shirts, we will look really cool racing around the track."

"When kids see us riding down the street, we will look awesome! Every kid that sees us will want to have a bike and belong to our group."

When Matt and Nik rolled onto the track together, Josh and Doug stopped talking mid-sentence. "Look at you!" Doug said. "Your bike finally came. The silver looks really cool. I was afraid that you were so intrigued with Miss Wheelchair USA that you may have ordered a glittery, pink one."

When the boys quit laughing, Josh said, "By the way! I talked with the guy who builds bikes in his shop. I told him about our club and what we're trying to achieve. He's excited and asked if he can visit and meet the kids and families. He can bring some samples of his bikes for the families to see. He said he can adapt a bike for just about any ability."

"Good job, Josh! I feel like our Club is helping the kids and the community," Nik punched Josh in the arm. "It is amazing how you can channel your energy to get the job done. I'm sure glad that you're in our Club."

Matt rolled his new bike up and down the driveway. "This is so much cooler than my wheelchair. Let's ride, guys! I'm so ready to be as cool as Nik and Doug."

"Matt! You are the coolest guy I know," said Nik. "Let's roll!"

The boys decided to leave the track and ride down the street. Everyone waved, and every kid stared. The boys felt like Super Stars for a few minutes.

"Hey, guys! I gotta get home before dark. This has been a blast!" The boys waved as Nik rolled towards home.

"We better get home, too!" Matt said. "I don't want my Mom to worry, because this is the first time that I've taken the bike out."

As Matt rolled home, he was thinking about how much his life had changed since coming to this little town. There were no real strangers. Every person he had met had been helpful and friendly. He had never felt that he was surrounded by friends in St. Louis. This was a good place to heal and plan for the future.

Nik told his parents about Matt's new bike and their cruise around the neighborhood. "It was so much fun riding with the guys. I never felt like I belonged with any group before. It's really nice having friends."

"You are a very lucky young man, Nik," said his Dad. "Not everyone gets to have friends they can depend on. You guys really make a great team. I can just imagine a very bright future for you all."

20

Nik, Matt, and Doug decided to ask a couple of the guys who were pretty fast to join them in a race around the track. The chairs could not keep up with the bikes. But they all laughed because it was the fastest they had ever gone. Nik told them that someday they might get bikes and then they could really fly, too.

"Most won't get bikes," Matt replied. "But, it could give them a goal to strive for. I know when they see me get in and out of my car, they are impressed. We are giving them all hope and dreams."

Nik was thinking out loud. "Maybe, if we could get that bike company to donate a bike, it might really be an incentive for the boys and the girls. We could have some kind of a challenge to win it."

"Well," Matt said, "It could be whoever has the most awards by the end of the year. But then the kids who can't do a lot may think it's hopeless and give up. What if, just each week when they come to the meeting, they put their name in a box? At the end of the year, a name is drawn and everyone has an equal chance to win."

"I like that plan," Nik said. "It would be good advertising for the bike shop, too!"

Matt thought about it for a minute. "It could get the kids excited, and they would try to make every meeting to get their names in the box. It's only been a few weeks, and they are already stronger and getting more competitive. I love it when I hear them setting goals to achieve."

"You know," Nik said with a smile. "I think the parents are as excited as the kids. I don't think they ever thought their kids could belong to something that would be really good for them and give them friends. I think our whole community will benefit. They'll be more supportive and they'll be more accepting. I really enjoy seeing how our community has stepped up and become involved."

Matt laughed, "You know what, Nik? Maybe you'll become an ambassador. You're good at smoothing ruffled feathers, and you like helping people. I would vote for you."

"When the Board sees what we're doing, I bet they'll agree to keep our club going," said Matt. "I see only positive stuff happening here. I think they will decide that we are good for the kids and the school."

Nik's parents walked over to see what was keeping the boys.

"Nik, Buddy still has to get walked. You can't just leave him alone all the time. Maybe he can come with us next week. I think the kids would enjoy him. I know that he would enjoy the attention."

"Okay! Let's roll out. We have accomplished a lot today."

"Hey, Matt! Be sure to check with your Granddad about our ideas!"

"Sure thing!" Matt said as he slid into his car. "Let's go home. I'm starving!"

Nik's Mom laughed. "You guys are always starving."

Buddy met them at the door, with his leash in his mouth.

"I'm sorry, boy! Next week you can come with us. Let's go for a walk!"

The only negative to taking Buddy to the Club Meeting was that he wanted to run with everyone. He did not like sitting while the kids were running or racing their chairs. He got so excited that he almost tipped over Nik's chair.

Mom took the leash and took Buddy for a walk. When they came back, she suggested leaving Buddy home next time. It would have been a good idea, except Buddy was used to being on the farm, where he could run and play and work.

"When we're done here, can Buddy and I go running at the park?" asked Josh. "I can help him burn up some energy."

Mom smiled, "I'm sure he would love that."

"I'm trying to talk my Dad into getting a dog. I spend a lot of time alone, and I think a dog would be good company," Josh explained. "I think you guys probably get tired of me always hanging out at your house."

"Josh, you and Nik are best friends. He would be lonely if you didn't come over. You are like my bonus son. You are always welcome at our home. Since Nik's big brothers grew up and got families of their own, I'm sure he enjoys having his best friend to hang out with."

"Thanks! That means a lot to me. I've never had a brother. I guess Nik is a brother in a lot of ways. I wouldn't have nearly as much fun without him. Ha! Ha! I would probably get into more trouble sitting home by myself."

Nik sat out by the driveway, hitting his tetherball. Sometimes it was nice to do nothing for a while. He could hear Buddy barking at the kitchen door.

"Okay, Buddy! Let's take a walk, and then you can play in the sprinklers."

Mom watched from her workshop window. "I wonder what Nik has on his mind. He doesn't usually mess with the tetherball unless he's worrying about something."

She watched as Nik and Buddy headed for the sprinklers. Who would have thought they would enjoy the sprinklers so much! Maybe it was because they could play together and cool off.

When Nik rolled into the house, he went right to his room to get ready for a shower. Nik decided that he would rather take a relaxing bubble bath.

When he was ready to face the world again, Nik rolled into the kitchen. "Something smells good. Whatcha cookin? Shall I set the table?"

"Well, I guess a bubble bath makes you feel better. Are you worried about something, Nik? You looked worried and deep in thought when I saw you outside. That's about the only time you hit the ball."

"I'm okay. I was just thinking that we haven't seen Grandma this summer. Is she okay? Can we visit her, or can she come visit us? My summer just doesn't feel right without spending time with her."

"You're right, Nik! I would really like to see my Mom. She hasn't been feeling very well, but I will call to see what she would like to do. It would probably make her feel better to spend some time with the people who love her. I'm sure Buddy would love to see her."

Nik and his Mom were getting Grandma's room ready, while Dad drove down to pick her up. "How long is she staying? I wish we could keep her with us all the time. I'm afraid we'll lose her and she won't know how much we love her."

Mom walked over to put her arms around Nik's shoulders. "I guess we share the same fears, sweetheart. I know in my heart that we will lose her one of these days. So, let's make sure she knows how much we love her while we have her."

"I can't imagine anything worse than losing your Mom or Dad," Nik whispered. "I'll be here if you need me, Mom!"

"Oh, my sweet boy! You know that everything that is born will die someday. No one knows when or how. We just have to love the people in our lives while we have them. The love of our family and friends helps us get through the tough times. Our faith in God gives us the strength to carry on."

"I hear the car! Grandma's here!"

Buddy was barking and dancing underfoot. Mom put him in the garage until Grandma could get inside and settled on the couch. When the garage door was opened, Buddy flew straight for Grandma. Grandma hugged him, and Buddy kissed her all over her face.

Nik rolled in to get his hugs and kisses. Mom and Dad watched with smiles and tears. "These are the moments to treasure. Take some pictures, please!" As she wiped her tears, Dad gave her a hug and started videotaping.

"How are you feeling, Grandma? Tomorrow we have our Club meeting. Would you like to watch the sports? You can use my extra chair if you need it."

"Nik, that sounds wonderful. I want to see and hear all about this new adventure of yours. You always keep my life from being boring."

Nik looked at his Mom. "What's for dinner? We're starving!"

When Nik's Grandma sat on her walker seat to watch the Club activities, she was amazed at what all the kids tried to accomplish.

She and Nik's Mom sat and laughed and cheered for each kid to do their best. "My dear, how in the world did you guys ever come up with this idea? These kids are laughing and cheering each other on. I am so impressed."

"Well, Mom!" Nik's Mom replied. "This is all because Nik and his friends wanted to give other kids a chance to experience some of what they got to do at camp. They learned a lot at camp about what other kids don't get to experience here in our country, but also around the world. It was a real wake-up call for them. They came home, ready to change the world. I think every kid and family around here will benefit."

Grandma smiled. "That's our Nik! He just has to bring fun and joy to everyone he meets. I'm very proud of him."

22

On Saturday, Mr. Peterson and the boys were sitting under a shade tree at the park. "Are you guys satisfied with how things are going?"

Josh laughed. "I think everyone is having fun. Every week, the kids are getting stronger and faster."

"Yes," Nik said. "But some of the kids have other events that they participate in at Special Olympics, that we haven't started yet. Mr. Peterson, do you think the park would let us have some swimming and diving practices? I heard some of the parents say that what we're doing isn't helping the swimmers."

"Well, I can check with the Director," Mr. Peterson said. "I don't think there'll be a problem. They have the Life Guards and Instructors who could help with learning skills. I think that when I tell them what we're doing, they will want to be involved."

"Cool!" said Matt. "Swimming is an excellent exercise. Even kids who aren't swimmers can learn a new skill. We could have a party at the end of the season. Wouldn't it be fun to have a Luau?"

Mr. Peterson laughed. "You guys are certainly full of ideas. It will be nice to offer something a little different for a while. I'll have to put together some ideas for swimming and diving contests. I will let you know what the Director says."

"What else can we add to our program?" Nik asked. "We need to have a variety of events to work on. We don't want people to get bored. If we try something new every few weeks, they'll stay excited."

Matt sat thinking for a few minutes. "We have a list of all the events that everyone gave us when we started. Let's look them over and see if there's things that we can work into our program. We could check with Reni, too. She has a good handle on the girls' events."

When the boys met up with Mr. Peterson, he let them know that they could start swimming in two weeks. "You will have to announce it at the meeting tonight, so people have time to prepare."

"What will it cost?" Nik asked. "Some of these kids don't have much money."

"It just so happens that the school will cover the cost. They were given a grant to provide more services for the kids with challenges. We'll have to give a written report on what the money was used for and how we think it went. Like, did we see progress or have any problems."

Mr. Peterson laughed. "They have no idea that these guys are just having fun while gaining skills."

"Why don't we have a pool at our school?" Josh asked. "Most of the other schools have pools."

Mr. Peterson smiled, "You have to remember that we are a small school. With the park right next door, it works pretty good for us. It's just not very useful in the winter."

"I guess that's why our Special Olympics has those competitions at the larger schools," Nik said. "I guess we're lucky that our events can compete on the track."

"We are lucky," Mr. Peterson replied. "We don't have to bus everyone to the city. Other than not having a pool, we do pretty good."

Matt sat quietly listening. "If we got the funding, could we get a pool?"

"I don't think the District would approve it," Mr. Peterson answered. "The Education Department would have a hard time agreeing to a pool when all the rest of the school's needs are not getting met."

The boys shook their heads. Nik said, "It's pretty unfair if you ask me."

23

When the kids arrived at the pool, the director welcomed them. He explained the rules and courtesy policies. He gave them a tour and explained how everything worked.

"If someone needs help, just yell. The lifeguards and instructors are here to help you and keep you safe. A lot of you have been here before. Help your friends out."

"Now, Mr. Peterson. Tell me what we can do to help you out."

The kids were divided by their experience level. The Special Olympics swimmers knew what they needed to practice. There were only two who needed to learn to swim. Everyone was tested to check their swimming skills.

"Okay, guys!" Mr. Peterson announced before everyone went home. "Next week we'll have some contests and maybe play some water volleyball."

Matt watched his Grandfather pack things up. "Gramps, let me carry some of that stuff. You've worked all day, and then you came here to help us. We appreciate everything you do. But, please let me give you a hand."

"Okay. Help yourself!"

"The families seemed to have a good time this evening. I guess I hadn't thought about swimming as important as racing and other physical things we do. I'm glad that Nik was listening to the families."

"Well, Matt! Football, basketball, and wrestling have always been our sports. I guess we have to broaden our horizons and learn about some other sports. We will do fine. If not, the parents will straighten us out. They all want to have little Champions."

Most of the families sat and cheered as the kids learned to swim and dive. Some of the parents were in the water helping with activities.

When Mr. Peterson put the net across the pool and announced that it was volleyball time, everyone was excited. The kids who had just learned to swim stayed at the shallow end of the pool. Some of the parents were on the teams playing, and some were stationed around the pool to keep an eye out for any problems.

Matt hit the first ball out over the net. Two boys jumped for it, and they both went underwater, missing the ball. They came up laughing. Both teams laughed and missed most balls. No one really cared. They were having a blast just having fun.

Mr. Peterson decided that not every event had to teach a skill. Some events should just let kids be kids and have fun. None of these kids had ever gotten to have so much fun.

The following week, they had races in the pool. Some of the kids were pretty fast, some struggled. But each week, they got stronger and braver.

The families all agreed that the swimming events were great for all the kids. Even the kids who didn't participate in the swimming events at Special Olympics had all learned skills and had so much fun with their friends.

The last evening for swimming was a warm, beautiful day with an awesome sunset. Matt had picked up grass skirts, leis, and tropical music. All the families brought dishes to pass.

As the mothers set up the food, Matt got the music playing. It was a very fun evening with friends. A very nice way to end the summer swimming.

Awards were handed out, and very special thank-you gifts for all the volunteers. Mr. Peterson told everyone what a great job they had done.

"School is starting soon, so we will be back at school in the gym for our activities. We will be doing some joint activities with our regular sports teams. As long as you do your best, we are happy. These young people have been working out and training for years. I think you can learn from each other."

"Be sure to wear your Club t-shirts to show your patches and pins. You have earned them, and I am proud of each one of you. Thank you, parents, for all your work and support. Without you, we couldn't have done this."

The music was still playing as people headed home.

"What a delightful evening!" Nik's Mom said as she packed things to go home. "I don't think we could find a better group of friends anywhere." Dad agreed, and they all headed home.

24

"Gee, guys!" Reni commented as she ran up the steps to the deck. "Every time I see you, you're eating. Oh! What kind of pizza is that? Maybe I'll have just one piece. It smells so good!"

"Yeah, Mom and Dad went out for the evening. So, they ordered pizza for us. Drinks are in the fridge. Where ya been?"

"Oh, the girls decided to go shopping. I had nothing better to do. I told Mom where I was going."

"That's okay! We just decided to have a little round table discussion about the club to see if we need to adjust or change anything. You can join us and give us your opinion or ideas."

"Thanks, guys!" Reni sat down with a drink to join the group. "I do have some ideas. Go on with your discussion, and I will jump in when I have something to say."

Josh started the discussion. "You know that some of the regular athletes are coming to volunteer. But what if we set up some little competitions with them and our athletes? They would all benefit and learn from each other. Maybe our guys would work a little harder. It could help the athletes become friends."

Nik said, "I like that idea. What if we ask some of them to become mentors? Everyone needs a friend to encourage and cheer them on. Someone who would pick them up if they fell. That way, our competitions would stay friendly and fun."

91

Reni decided that it was time for her to speak up.

"Most of my young ladies want to have fun. There's a lot of giggling and laughing. But if they were competing with regular athletes, it might make them take this more seriously and try harder. Having a mentor might really encourage them."

"Okay! I'll talk to Gramps and see what he thinks. I bet he will like the idea. Maybe it's time to have some competitions with the parents."

The next morning, on the way to school, the boys discussed how they could get more kids involved.

Nik suggested that they could advertise in the school paper that they were looking for students to be mentors for the Club Members. "We would have to be careful to only let kids who really cared to get involved. We don't want anyone who might tease them or not be respectful."

"I think Gramps should be the deciding person for the mentors. He knows most of the students. He knows their personalities and how they behave and how they treat people," Matt said, thoughtfully.

"I think most of our students here are really great," Josh said. "But some can be a bit of a bully. I've never seen anyone be really mean, but we don't want anything to go wrong for our guys."

As the boys rolled up to school, they were greeted by a lot of old and new friends. Nik said, "We certainly know more kids this year than we did last year."

"It's funny," Josh said. "I feel like a lot more people like me."

"You know, Josh," Nik said. "In the last year, I think we've grown up a lot. You don't joke as much. You can be very serious and think through your problems better. I think we have all matured a lot."

Matt laughed, "For sure, you don't act like goofy kids no more. Everyone respects you more for helping other kids so much. I know my Grandpa is impressed with you all."

"We better get to class or we're going to get yelled at," said Nik.

25

When Nik rolled into Homeroom, his teacher gave him a note, telling him to go to the office.

Oh, boy! Nik wondered if he had broken a rule or forgotten something important. He worried that they might shut down his club.

"Well, Nik," the Principal said from behind his desk. He looked pretty intimidating and powerful. He stood up and walked around his desk. He sat in a chair that put him eye to eye with Nik.

"I have some really good news for you and your friends. We have been getting some very positive reports from parents and other students about your club. Parents are calling to thank us for this wonderful new program. Some of the school neighbors have been calling us to say how much they are enjoying watching our special kids in their competitions."

"I have to tell them that it wasn't my idea and that a group of students dreamed it up. They all think it's great, and so does the School Board. We have decided that we don't need three months to watch your progress. You have our approval and support as long as everything goes well. If there's any kind of problem, let me know before it turns into a big problem."

"We think it's such a good idea that we are going to recommend it to all our schools in our district. We feel that it's a real asset to our school."

"Holy cow!" Nik exclaimed. "Who would have thought we were going to have so much success this fast? Thank you! We have only just begun! We have so much that we want to do. We have so many ideas! We want all the kids to feel like Champions! They are working so hard and having so much fun."

"When we have our next District Meeting," the Principal asked, "Would it be possible for your Team to present your plans and results so far to our committee? I think they will be pretty impressed with what you and your friends have achieved."

"Sure, I guess so!" Nik replied. "Let me talk with Mr. Peterson, my team, and my parents. But, I don't think there will be a problem."

"Very good, Nik! Here's a hall pass so you can get back to class."

When Nik rolled into class, he was smiling and could barely wait until he could tell Josh the good news.

"What happened?" whispered Josh.

"I'll tell you after class," Nik said. "It's all good news!"

Josh caught up with Nik just as they entered the gym.

"Mr. Peterson!" Nik called out as he rolled up beside him. "You are not going to believe what the Principal told me!"

Mr. Peterson watched the boys as he wiped his hands on the towel that always hung from his back pocket.

"Well, gentlemen, what has gotten you excited?"

Nik explained, "I got called to the Principal's Office. I thought I might be in trouble. But, it was actually good news."

"The School Board has heard such good reports about our club, they have decided that we don't have to wait three months for their approval. As long as everything goes well, we have been approved to keep going. Parents and school neighbors have been calling to say how much they are enjoying watching our teams compete."

"Also, they want us to go to the next district meeting to tell the other schools about what we are doing. They would like all the schools to come up with a program like ours. They would like the other schools to offer an avenue to help special needs students to grow and give the regular students a chance to be involved."

"He's really impressed with how we've gotten all our students involved together. The Principal wants us to give a talk and show what we have accomplished."

"I know you guys are doing great stuff, but I am amazed that the school is so supportive. This is pretty unusual!" Mr. Peterson stopped to wipe his hands a little more. "I love seeing the joy on the kids' faces. This has got to be one of my favorite projects that I have been involved with. Boys, you are changing lives in a very good way."

"Let's get our group together and lay out an outline, so we can put together a presentation that will knock their socks off."

97

26

Every week, every member showed up, bubbling with excitement. Each week a few more families came to check them out. They had to make sure their kids would fit in and be safe.

The parents discovered that the club was as much for them as it was for the kids. They found friendships and support, which they had never had before.

As the group grew, they started splitting into groups for specific sports. They would all be involved with every sport in their group. Watching everyone improve their skills showed the boys that their idea was a success.

When Reni set her team of girls up for competitions, there was laughter and giggling. The boys watched, but they couldn't see what was so funny. It made no sense to them. Reni was so impressed that the girls were not overly competitive or jealous. Each one cheered on all her friends to do their best.

Mr. Peterson and Nik's Dad sat and watched all the activities. Mr. Peterson said, "I have never worked with a group of kids that had more fun and cheerfulness than this group. Even if they fall or tip over, they just laugh and get back in the game."

Nik's Dad laughed, "You know, even your regular athletes are having a blast. This is like a mini Special Olympics every week."

Nik's Mom volunteered to hand out the Medals and patches for improvements and for helping others. Some of the t-shirts were getting their shields pretty decorated.

Mr. Peterson said, "By the way, next week is the District Board Meeting. Do you think the boys have their presentation ready?"

"Oh, my goodness!" Nik's Mom laughed. "They are really going to impress that Committee. They have a couple parents lined up to talk about their kids' achievements. They have a couple of the older boys lined up to give their opinion of the club. The boys themselves are presenting facts and figures to prove how successful the Club has become. As their Head Coach, will you have something to add?"

"I think the boys have this pretty well put together. I'll be there in case there's questions they can't answer," Mr. Peterson smiled. "I think we will be well represented. Everyone will wear their Knights' Quest t-shirts, and they're having everyone show up as one big Team."

Mr. Peterson laughed, "They will not forget these kids and their enthusiasm. I am so proud of them."

27

When the doors swung open for the District School Board Meeting, the room was filled.

Half the Football Team and Cheerleaders walked in behind the wheelchairs and other Club Members and their parents.

All the District School Board Members took notice that the room was filled to overflowing. They had expected a couple of speakers, but not a crowd. This time, there were no complaints or demands.

Mr. Peterson stepped up to the mic first. He told the assembly of school representatives that he had coached regular sports teams for thirty years. But, he had never seen the excitement and determination like these Special Needs kids and parents. He introduced his young friends and sat down.

Parents stepped up to tell how their sons and daughters had overcome fears and felt like they belonged to an awesome group of friends who encouraged them to be their best at whatever was coming.

Physically, they were improving, their school grades were improving, and they were happy and excited about their lives and their friends. This had never happened before.

They all recommended that other schools offer similar experiences to help their Special Needs students.

When all the speakers were done, the Football Captain asked if he could say a few words.

"Ladies and Gentlemen, my team and I would like to thank you all for letting us be a part of this experience. We have all seen these guys grow and overcome fears, and gain strength and skills. It makes us feel like we have never really put all our hearts into our games and cared about each other enough. These kids have taught us to be better athletes and human beings."

After a standing ovation, the Board President spoke.

"My goodness! We had no idea that a group of kids in wheelchairs could do what we'd say, *'Good job, kids! Bring forth this kind of achievement.'* We were originally thinking that we'd say *'Good job, kids. Keep up the good work.'* But, we have decided that we would like to use your club as a role model for all the schools in our District. You never know, maybe at some point we'll have some competitions between our schools, other than Special Olympics. Thank you all for showing us what true community and sportsmanship should be like."

"Can you believe how our support group came out for us tonight?" Nik asked as his parents helped him get ready for bed. Between yawns, he asked, "Wouldn't it be great if every school had their own club? It would really improve those kids' lives and their families."

Mom and Dad left Nik with smiles on their faces.

Dad said, "What do you think he will come up with tomorrow?"

Mom chuckled. "Only God knows. But, like Nik says, tomorrow's a new day, and you know, he will make it interesting."

About the Author

Beth Watter grew up in the Missouri Ozarks and moved to Illinois at 16. After graduating from Freeport High School, she attended Highland College and spent two years at a New England Literature School. She married her high school sweetheart, Klaus, and they had three sons. Their youngest, Nik, was born with a heart defect, and after a life-threatening surgery, he developed cerebral palsy. Beth spent years helping him through his recovery and supporting him in earning his Eagle Scout.

Inspired by her journey, Beth turned to writing to encourage other families to stay strong and chase their dreams.